Canine
Capers

**Life's Delights and Dilemmas
through Dogs' Eyes**

Sally Hurst

Publications

Canine Capers

British Library Cataloguing-in-Publication Data.

A catalogue record for this book is available from The British Library.

ISBN: 978-1-913579-41-8 (Paperback)
ISBN: 978-1-913579-42-5 (ebook)

Publisher: Ladey Adey Publications, Copperhill, 1 Ermine Street, Ancaster, Lincolnshire, NG32 3PL, UK.

Cover Picture adapted from a photograph by David Newman Spherical Photography.

Illustrations adapted by Abbirose Adey from photographs taken by Sally Hurst, Phil Speed and David Newman.

The Author has done everything to ensure accreditation of copyright of other's work. The Author accepts full responsibility for any errors or omissions.

The characters and events in this book are fictitious. The author does not intend any apparent similarity to actual persons or likenesses.

Ladey Adey Publications do not not have any control over, or any responsibility for, any author or third-party websites referred to in this book.

Contact the author via sallyhurst@live.com

If you enjoyed this book please add a review on Amazon for Sally.

Dedication

This book is dedicated to my mum, Sheila.
The most selfless person I have ever known...

... and to all the Jack Russell lovers
across the world.

Contents

Raison d'être

My book is a talking toolkit, set around two Jack Russells, which I hope will enable families to talk about difficult issues. This includes issues which affect their family members or family life. By acknowledging life's delights and dilemmas family members can reach out for help.

The 'Human Highlight' sections at the end of each chapter clarify the issues before moving onto discussion and dialogue questions called, 'Sniff It Out!'

The questions have been designed to open up conversations about the subjects featured in each chapter. They are open-ended questions which cannot be answered by just 'yes' or 'no', therefore help people to open up and talk about problems, issues or any worries.

Once dialogue has begun and where more help is needed, there is a comprehensive list of charities who can help with all the issues featured.

The book is written through the eyes of Apple and Maci, my Jack Russells. This is because dogs have an unpolluted view of life. They see the real person and the real picture; they give unconditional love which is sometimes lacking in our modern world.

I am a shameless dog lover and because of this I have included a chapter on Jack Russell traits and behaviour. This is to save dogs suffering unnecessarily simply because their owners have not considered the type of dog and its inherent traits which ideally suit their family.

The initial inspiration for this book came from seeing how my lovely Mum suffered in later life because her parents only communicated with her about the day-to-day aspects of life, never about her worries, dreams and aspirations in life. This left her lacking the ability to express her emotions, talk about or discuss issues which affected her, make friends and suffering from low self–esteem.

Canine Capers is designed to prevent this happening to anybody else. It is not only an icebreaker which facilitates the free flow of communication within families, but is a toolkit to help resolve problems.

It has been a great honour for me to write this book for my Mum, who is hopefully looking fondly down on us. Please take time to read this with your family and savour the conversations which will hopefully arise from it as you too consider life's delights and dilemmas through dogs' eyes.

Pregnancy

Snuggly and cosy - this is how we felt as we woke up and let out a great big yawn. We felt so safe and warm - nowhere could be any better as far as we were concerned.

It was a bit of a squash, but feeling the movements and heartbeats of our brothers and sisters was calming to us. The gentle undulating rhythm of Mummy's heartbeat was very soothing and relaxing.

Suddenly, our warm and cosy world changed; we were shocked and scared. Why it changed is a mystery to us, but in only a few moments we were no longer cocooned with our siblings in our calm, cosy, twilight world of Mummy's tummy, but wriggling on a warm, soft, cushiony object beside our Mummy.

We panicked. We could not feel our siblings' movements; thankfully though, we soon realised we could reach out and touch them. We had a lot more space and could now move about freely.

There was nothing better than cuddling up close to our Mummy. We felt the warmth of her body and her love as she fussed over us, licking us to keep us clean and making sure we could all get to her teats to drink her milk.

Guess what? We could now smell. Smells gatecrashed our previously odourless, dark and silent world. They forced their way in, shot up our nostrils and made our heads spin. Our brains were overloaded by the variety and intensity of them. Sometimes we tied ourselves up in knots trying to smell them all at once.

However, one constant, familiar and velvety smell reassured us whenever these new smells overwhelmed us. The wonderful smell of our family; Mummy, our brothers and our sisters.

Another of our favourite smells was Mummy's food. The tasty morsels she was given smelled delicious – they made our mouths water.

The smells came and went. There were regular smells at the beginning of the day and at the end of the day. Then there were smells which did not happen everyday. There was a very fragrant and clean smell, oily and greasy smells, smoky smells and downright weird smells!

However, our world was still silent... until one day when a cornucopia of noises began to intrude into our silent, still and mute lives.

Sound was the next of our senses to be awakened. Different noises appeared gradually and we were aware of the steady intensity of them. It was as if sound itself was being gentle with us and did not want to overwhelm us.

It started to be fun – we heard: Whoosh Whoosh, Ping Ping, Slosh Slosh, Thud Thud, Weeeeeeee, Hmmmmmmm... Hmmmmmmm. Some were loud and some were soft, some high pitched and some low pitched. Some were conversations which continued throughout the day. They came from all directions, we were fascinated. Only one final frontier to contend with. We could not see. It was frustrating, because we wanted to explore and find the fascinating noises and smells.

It is normal for us not to see when we are born (it can take up to two weeks), but when our eyes opened you can imagine how nosy and inquisitive we became.

It was exciting to discover what we looked like and what our Mummy looked like. We all looked similar, although Mummy was bigger than us. We weren't scared because we knew she loved us and was so cuddly.

We learnt where all the noises came from including the high and low pitched sounds. Non-doggies. Big ones and a small one. The non-doggies were fascinating. Not only did they walk on two legs – they were not covered in fur! They came in different sizes and we realised the small non-doggie was always very excited to see us and played with us.

Then disaster struck. Different large non-doggies came and took our siblings. We had no warning, no chance to say goodbye. We stayed close to our Mummy, as we did not want to get taken, too.

We think our mummy must have been sad because she often lay on her own and gazed sadly into space.

Human Highlight

🏃 *Possibly one of the most common things which parents dread is how and when to tell their children about 'the birds and the bees'. They ponder about how old they should be, how to broach the subject, do they wait until their children ask about it, how much detail to impart, what terms to use for those parts of the body, or do they simply wait until they receive sex education at school.*

🏃 *However, my view is that parents and guardians should not rely upon their children's school to provide a comprehensive sex education; there needs to be input from them especially in the case of questions which their children may be too embarrassed to ask in front of their classmates.*

🏃 *This chapter about pregnancy will hopefully help you open up dialogue about this important subject. Children are naturally curious about pregnancy and reproduction. The age of the child, will determine how you answer. A younger child may be happy with a simple factual answer. An older child may need more detail. It may help to ask them what they already know or think about the subject. If you need to discuss body parts remember to use the correct names and terminology.*

Sniff It Out!

🐕 What was the soft cushiony thing?

🐕 Where do dogs come from?

🐕 Where did you come from?

🐕 What is your first memory?

🐕 What smells could the puppies smell?

🐕 What smells do you like?

🐕 The puppies' Mummy fed and cleaned them. How do your parents look after you?

🐕 How did the doggies' bodies change as they got older.

🐕 How has your body changed as you have got older?

🐕 If you have brothers and sisters, how do you play or get along with them?

🐕 If you don't have siblings, then what do you like or dislike about being an only child?

New Home

One evening, two new non-doggies appeared - large ones again. They sat with the two big non-doggies we already knew and made the same noises the others made. Why were they here? Other large non-doggies had come and taken our brothers and sisters away - would these take us?

On this memorable evening, we were old enough to play out of sight of our Mum and we were playing very happily together, when our largest non-doggie suddenly picked us both up and passed us to the new non-doggies.

We were scared. We both trembled with trepidation. We could not see our Mummy. What are they going to do to us? Would anything bad happen to us?

Our emotions swirled like kaleidoscopes; whirling round and changing, morphing into every imaginable element of fear.

The worse thing was our Mummy was still not there. Did she know what was happening? Were they going to take us away like our brothers and sisters were taken away. Poor Mummy, we saw how forlorn this made her. How would our Mummy cope? We were the last of her babies. Would this totally destroy her?

However, we did not need to be afraid of these new non-doggies after all. Each of the new non-doggies tenderly stroked us. Then they kissed us. They were both so gentle with us. It was like being loved by our Mummy.

One of them popped out and came back with a big metal box. The next thing we knew was the small non-doggie person we knew and remembered from before we could see, was kissing us and saying goodbye. She looked sad as though she would miss us but was happy for us as we set upon our new adventure.

We were then put in the big metal box and lifted into an even bigger box with four wheels. HELP! There was a loud roaring sound and nasty vibrations - the box with wheels was moving. We clung onto each other for dear life. What was going to happen to us?

The roaring box full of nasty vibrations swung from side to side, making us slide about and this seemed to last for an eternity.

It eventually stopped. The big metal box we were in was lifted out and carried into an even bigger box made of bricks - a house!

We escaped from the big metal box and started to explore - there were so many new smells to enjoy. The two new non-doggies followed us around, but we did not feel threatened by them. They were interested in what we were doing.

Extreme curiosity and excitement replaced our fear. Then, to add to our fun, we were led to food and water. The food smelled just as good as it did in our first home and there was plenty of water to drink, which we needed after all of our exploring!

The next morning, we woke up in our new home in our own bedroom which was part of our new non-doggies bedroom. They had made it cosy for us with snuggly, quilts and blankets to sleep on and water nearby in case we were thirsty during the night.

The bedroom door opened and we stepped out carefully. The non-doggies led us to a big room with a comfy thing like the one we used to sit on in our first home. We sniffed around a lot to make sure it was the same room we had been in the previous night - it was.

Then something clever happened. A big glass wall was pushed open and we walked through the opening.

The floor felt different under our paws - strange. It was not soft like the floor in the big room. Ooh! What was the green tufty stuff? It tickled our noses. We stepped from the hard surface onto it. It was soft and springy.

The non-doggies were very patient with us and let us explore the lay of the land at our own pace. This new place had walls but no ceiling it kept going up and up - we wondered why? Our next step was to suss out the bushy objects made up of different shapes and colours.

Lots were green but they all had different shaped leaves in lots of different colours: white, red, pink, orange and yellow - a mixture! When the non-doggies were not looking we nibbled one of the leaves. Yuk!

What about the different coloured clusters? One smelled like one of the non-doggies but another did not smell of anything.

Achoo! Something got stuck on our noses. Achoo! Achoo! It was all powdery.

Buzz! Buzz! Ooh! Fuzzy buzzy creatures which we followed but the non-doggies warned us not to eat them – they called them bees and explained they help the bushy things called flowers and plants to grow.

The plants were coming out of crumbly brown stuff. This was interesting and worth further investigation. Our paws slightly sunk into it. Hmmmm, could we move it with our paws? Wow! Yes! We had to dig and make a hole! Now, we had somewhere to bury precious things and keep them safe – excellent!

Something cool brushed against us but we could not see it. It brushed against us again and again. It was strange: we had no idea what it could be, but we could see it brushing past the leaves too and making them move. The non-doggies called it the wind.

In the sky, there was a yellow ball which threw down warmth into the garden. It was a very strange but interesting room – which we needed to investigate more.

This room felt good to be in; with the fresh smells, the breeze and the radiating heat from the yellow ball. The non-doggies kept saying *"Do you like the garden?"* So, this was what this fantastic room was called!

There were other creatures who visited our garden. One creature was the thing with wings. We had seen similar creatures before, but these would land in the garden and peck at the lawn. We were cross about this. They did not ask our permission to land in OUR garden. We barked at them - Ha! this made them fly away.

But, the four legged animals with long, snaky tails and whiskers were the worst. They nonchalantly entered the garden; climbing up and over the fence. How did they do that? What were they? The non-doggies told us they were cats.

Luckily, the non-doggies did not mind us barking or chasing (but not hurting) the cats - they did not like them coming into the garden either because they sometimes did a poo amongst our plants!

Between chasing the things with wings and the cats; we stretched out and enjoyed a rest in the warmth of the sun, which is what the yellow ball in the sky is.

Some plants in the garden were pretty and others not so pretty. The green tufty stuff was grass and made a lawn. The pretty colourful plants were called flowers. The others were vegetables.

We were astonished when we first saw the non-doggies pull a plant out of the earth and hold it in the air like a trophy, with the earth still clinging to its roots - then they ate it for their dinner! Our food comes from a bag, pouch or tin.

We loved exploring the garden because there was more space than in the room with the comfy seats. Furthermore, the feeling of the lawn on your back while doing a roly-poly is magical!

We played with our toys, played games with each other and sniffed the lawn, soil and vegetable beds incessantly, although the non-doggies did not like it when we jumped into the vegetable beds!

All in all, we were impressed with our new home. The furniture did not match and was old, but it was clean and cosy; warm and welcoming. Some objects were too high for us to jump onto ourselves, but we had already developed our doe-eyed look which meant the non-doggies lifted us up; how good is that!

They let us sit on the settee with them and did not mind our hairs getting all over them!

Our home was small, but the garden was big, and we just loved running around it.

We concluded a home does not need to be all posh with brand new furniture. It is more important for it to be comfortable, welcoming and relaxing.

The new non-doggies were very kind and welcoming too and they gave us new names, Apple and Maci. We were also very pleased with our names and decided we would adopt the non-doggies as our new mummy and daddy!

Human Highlight

🚶 *Sometimes life can change very suddenly and for no obvious reason, which can really pull the rug out from under our feet. Change can feel scary, especially to young children who may not have any coping mechanisms, yet in place.*

🚶 *In this chapter, Apple and Maci are taken to a new home and away from their birth mother. As you may have noticed from the arrival and description of their first few days in their new home, not all change is negative and can be exciting and joyful as they explore outside too.*

🚶 *This chapter is designed to approach the subject of new places or change as an adventure and a positive experience. There may be acceptable elements of risk with unknown places or things, however, if they are explained and understood, they can be utilised in a very positive way.*

Sniff It Out!

- What feelings did the puppies have when they arrived at their new home?

- What new things did they find?

- Can you describe your home?

- How do you feel when you are at home?

- What do you like most about your home?

- What is your first memory of your home?

- Why are the puppies given a new home? Is this different to humans?

- When do humans leave home without their parents

- What did the puppies notice in the garden?

- If you have a garden, what is it like?

- Do you have plants in your garden, can you name any of them and which are your favourite ones?

- Can plants be grown in different places?

- What do plants need to be healthy and strong?

- Where does your name come from?

- If you could choose your own name what would it be?

Our New Mummy & Daddy

Our new Daddy has a very deep and booming voice and our new Mummy has a higher and loud voice.

We did find this a bit scary at first, but we learned daddies usually do have deeper voices than mummies. We also discovered Mummy could not help having a loud voice. Daddy jokingly told us, *"Mummy has no volume control."* We knew he was telling the truth because we could not find it either!

As the days rolled by, we grew more and more confident in our new home. We loved to play everywhere – it was great being much smaller than our parents; we could play where they couldn't, like under the book case.

Our parents also let us play with them. They even let us jump all over them and lick them, which made us feel great. But we realised how much they loved us when they would let us fall asleep on them and did not move in case they woke us up, just like our doggie mummy used to. They would tell us, what good girls we were and how much they loved us, all while kissing us. It made us feel wanted and loved.

The penny dropped one day when we realised this was our new home. Our doggie Mummy still had a big space in our hearts and we hoped she had recovered from our departure. We also had fond memories of our first non-doggie family, but our new Mummy and Daddy were ours forever!

The only puzzle for us was why our new Mummy and Daddy took us away and why we were not able to stay with our Mummy but we knew we could visit if we wanted.

We must admit, we did have a few accidents on the carpet, but Mummy and Daddy understood. They would just clear it up and gently put us outside in the garden to show us where they wanted us to do our wees and poos.

Mummy and Daddy never shouted at us when we had accidents, but they did praise us when we asked to go out and did our business in the garden.

This kind of encouragement really helped us and did not make us feel naughty or upset. Mummy and Daddy understood it was something we needed time to learn. They were patient and understanding with us.

Their attitude built up our confidence and when we got it right, we trotted back inside with our tails held high and full of pride.

Human Highlight

🐾 *'Never judge a book by its cover' is an old but very wise saying and one which is reflected on in the description of Apple and Maci's new parents. Their initial fears are overcome as they become accustomed to their new parents and new home and understand how much they are loved.*

🐾 *It is also important to understand we all have lessons to learn; toilet training, maths or how to get along with people. In this chapter, success by the dogs in their training is rewarded rather than failure punished. The message is rewards for good behaviour work well. Punishment often exacerbates problems by making children nervous and in severe cases traumatising children who may then have problems in later life. A child's confidence increases with praise. Without fear of punishment or ridicule, they may find it easier to talk about issues which they find embarrassing or difficult.*

ᛡᛡ *This chapter provides a chance to approach new events children have experienced and how they coped with them. Or if they are still struggling, discussing ways to build resilience and strength.*

Sniff It Out!

🐾 *Where do you go to the loo? Is it different to where the puppies go?*

🐾 *What new things did you have to learn?*

🐾 *Are there things you are still trying to learn?*

🐾 *How do your parents/carers make you feel?*

🐾 *How would you describe your parents or carers? What are their qualities?*

🐾 *Which qualities do your parents/carers teach you, for example, accepting people for who they are?*

🐾 *Are there things you wish you could say to your parents/carers, but the subject makes you feel too embarrassed?*

🐾 *If you have had to leave a parent or care-giver, how do you feel about it?*

Our First Walk

We loved the garden and were very happy to play there. It had not occurred to us that there was more to explore outside of the garden, until the memorable day of our first walk.

When we heard the word 'walk' for the first time, we did not know what it meant. We soon found out and discovered how much fun we would have!

Mummy and Daddy put these strange things

round our necks called collars; (we were not keen on them) they felt strange. We soon realised however we would have to cope with wearing them. On each collar was a loop to attach a lead. The lead was a rope held by our Mummy or Daddy so we would walk close to them.

Off we went – through the door and out onto the driveway and beyond our house. It was called outside – outside of our home and garden. It was not at all scary, it was just different. There were lots of houses, with gardens, trees and more of the green tufty stuff.

There was chirping in the trees from the winged creatures: Mummy and Daddy did not mind them in these trees. They made very musical sounds. Sometimes, it seemed as though they were talking to each other and sometimes the tweets sounded like song. We guessed they communicated with each other just like we did.

But, WOWZA! There were more new smells. This was the best bit! The new smells danced merrily about in our noses. We did not know where they all came from, but remembering how our mum and siblings smelled, we guessed they were of other dogs.

They came from everywhere and we pulled on our leads to smell them all: to find out where they were coming from. We could smell the other dogs in the air and on the green tufty stuff which we now knew was grass.

This is when we discovered why our collars and leads were very important. They kept us close to Mummy and Daddy, so they could watch us and keep us safe. They stopped us from walking into a road, where the large, noisy, metal things with four wheels are. If one of those drove over us we would be squashed and hurt.

As we walked around the corner, we were grateful to have Mummy and Daddy so near to us, because we encountered non-doggies whom we had not seen before and they had a doggie too.

We stopped. Would these non-doggies be nice? Could we trust them like we did our parents? What about their doggie. It was bigger than us and it made us nervous.

After our initial shock, we relaxed because our parents talked to the other non-doggies. Our Mummy bent down and stroked the other doggie - it wagged its tail, obviously enjoying the fuss our mummy made of it. We wondered if we ought to speak to it. We gave each other an inquisitive glance.

Whilst we were contemplating our next move, Mummy allowed the other dog to approach us. We stood our ground whilst he sniffed us. He was wagging his tail, so we thought it was a good sign because we wag our tails when we are happy or excited. We were not sure what we should do, but our instincts took over and we sniffed back.

BINGO!

One of the doggie smells we had experienced when we first got outside was his smell, so he must live near to us. He seemed OK, so we agreed he could be our doggie friend.

Human Highlight

ᛘ *Being adventurous is healthy and heading outside, either in the garden or further afield, can boost your feel-good hormones. However, it is important to ensure you are careful when visiting new places and making new friends and do not put yourself in dangerous situations. Apple and Maci's human parents knew they would not understand the risks and helped them stay safe by using collars and leads.*

ᛘ *Children, and adults, should also take precautions when heading out by letting a loved one know where they are going and when they expect to be back.*

ᛘ *This chapter provides an opportunity to discuss the joys of exercise, being outside with nature and how to stay safe outdoors.*

Sniff It Out!

🐕 Do you enjoy being outside? Why?

🐕 Where is your favourite walk or outside place?

🐕 Where do you play outside or go for walks?

🐕 Why did the dogs not go outside the garden immediately?

🐕 Do you have pets which you take for a walk?

🐕 How do you keep you and your pets safe when you are out for a walk?

🐕 Why do you think that going for walks is healthy for you? (Consider physical and mental benefits).

🐕 Who do you meet when you go outside and who goes out with you?

🐕 How do you feel about meeting other people with their dogs if you are out with your family? (Encourage canine awareness and respect of human and canine space.)

🐕 The puppies use their sense of smell to learn about new people and new things – how do you notice and learn new things?

Food
Glorious Food

Another set of smells which we love is food! We were familiar with the cooking smells in our first home. They usually drifted towards our noses three times a day. Our noses would start to gently twitch, so we would follow the tasty smelling trail and flop at the kitchen door, just in case.

Some smells were more tempting than others. The morning smells were not exciting and were usually generated by a clonk and a click – toast.

The aromas at the middle of the day, could also be mediocre. Sometimes, different things would be placed inside two slices of fluffy brown stuff and this really had a dull and bland smell.

A particularly interesting scent was from soup. Although this was food, it was poured into the bowls, like our water was poured into our drinking bowls: it was puzzling.

But, the most intriguing smells reached us in the evening. There was the hum of the oven, the sizzling of the frying pans and steam whooshing out of the saucepans.

Some of the aromas brought us to a state of rapture; yellow stuff was transformed into shreds when it was pushed against a metal gadget with holes in it, this was sprinkled on top of dishes and then they were put into the oven: thick slices of brown stuff were fried: white and red things which were peeled, sliced and also fried.

If only we could try some! Sometimes when Mummy or Daddy had turned the yellow stuff into shreds we got a couple of shreds each as a treat which was yummy.

However, our meals mostly consisted of dry food which came from a large tub. We did get healthy things mixed in with it, stuff called tuna and mackerel – we admit this was tasty and we enjoyed eating it. We knew they were healthy and good for us because our Mummy and Daddy told us.

One day, however, our luck turned. All of a sudden, we heard Mummy shriek out from the kitchen, *"Please no...oh no, oh no!"* and then she groaned. We could tell she was not injured, but something was wrong.

The kitchen door was not tightly shut, so we nudged it open to see what had befallen Mummy. *'Wow!'* we both thought, as our eyes popped out of our heads. There was food on the floor and there was some of the grated yellow stuff on it– yippee!

There was no time to waste. We wanted to help Mummy by eating it so she wouldn't have to clean the floor! However, our kind help was soon put to a stop.

Mummy shouted, *"Leave!"* and Daddy called us – we had to depart from our best meal ever! Our hearts sank, but we jumped up on the settee and both let out a long and deep sigh for what could have been...

Mummy and Daddy must have sensed we wanted to try more of their food as in the evening they had some of the thick slices of the solid brown stuff we had a few tiny bits mixed in with our food.

It was deee-li-cious! We licked our bowls so much they hardly needed to be washed up!

The only regret we had was they did not give us any of the white and red things which they ate with their thick slices of brown stuff. However, we did hear Mummy and Daddy talking as they put the flavoursome morsels into our bowls. Mummy said to Daddy, "Please make sure there is no onion (the white and red things), because it is not good for them."

Our sense of disappointment disappeared as we realised Mummy had not allowed us to eat the food on the floor because it had onions in it - she loves us so much.

Obviously, we always listened to Mummy and Daddy talking because we are naturally inquisitive. One day Mummy was on her rectangular device and she read out which foods are dangerous for dogs to eat.

It turned out the white and red things, onions, are dangerous for us to eat, as well as the red things, tomatoes, which they slice up to put between the slices of fluffy brown stuff. Even the sweet-smelling brown stuff, chocolate, which Mummy sometimes eats after her meal is dangerous to us dogs.

Thank goodness our Mummy and Daddy love us so much and take care to know which food is good for us and which is harmful to us.

We cannot eat the same food as Mummy and Daddy, so although our food does not always look as exciting as theirs, it is healthy for us which is why we feel so well!

They also coax us to eat if we do not touch our meals and prevent us from overeating by allowing us only a few treats and titbits.

We hope all Mummies and Daddies with doggies are knowledgeable about which food is good for non–doggies, which food is good for their doggies and how much food should be eaten.

Human Highlight

⚑ *Making healthy choices about what to eat can be difficult and varies from person to person and species to species. In this chapter, Apple and Maci learn some foods their human parents can eat are unsafe for them. This is also true of humans and many people have allergies or intolerances to certain foods.*

⚑ *This chapter opens discussion about food groups including how our food choices can effect our health, but also states that the occasional treat is okay. This can include where and how food is produced and also how children can grow their own fruit and vegetables.*

Sniff It Out!

- What foods do the dogs described in the story?

- Where does your food comes from?

- What's your favourite food/meal?

- Do you prefer sweet or savoury food?

- Can you name sweet and savoury food?

- Which food groups are the most healthy for you?

- Which types of food are good to have occasionally as a treat?

- Describe a time when you have eaten something even when you are not hungry. Why did you eat then?

- Describe a time when you refused to eat something. Why did you not want to eat it?

- Why should you not give dogs onions or chocolate?

- What different things can happen if you eat too much of the wrong foods?

Bullying

One lovely spring day we were out on a walk with our Mummy and Daddy. It was one of our favourite walks through the trees which were covered in blossom. The sun's rays warmed our bodies as they pierced through the lush, green foliage on the trees producing magical dappled strands of light which danced on the path.

Life could not be better. We loved our routine of two walks a day. We loved them because it meant we could go out, sniff oodles of things and see our doggie friends.

A new element of walks, which Maci cunningly introduced, is when she wants to change the direction of the walk, she simply stops. I, Apple, don't know how she does this; it's as if her paws are glued to the ground. Although we are small dogs, our strength is amazing; Maci demonstrates this in an exemplary fashion. I named this technique, *'Maci's Mutiny!'*

On this fateful day, Maci had pulled off another victory by directing us all to the park. Just like pirates find treasure, this was our greatest discovery. The grass was long and as smooth as satin. The trees provided shade when it was hot and there was great scope for sniffing.

We woofed, *"Hello!"* to our doggie friend, Max, as we bounded through the sweet smelling grass and continued to sniff up the mind-boggling abundance of smells.

Our euphoria was brought to a sudden, brutal and horrendous stop. A large dog called Titan whom we knew, but was not our friend, because he was very aggressive, had rushed over to Max and was attacking him.

He had pulled Max over onto his back and was attacking his neck and body. Titan was growling and bearing his large, sharp and dangerous looking teeth. Max growled back but also yelped in pain. If the attack had lasted any longer Max would not have survived. Titan was now pumped up on adrenalin and had tasted blood.

Max's Mummy was shouting, *"Help!"* over and over again. Luckily our Mummy and Daddy heard and rushed over, because she could not have coped on her own. Thank goodness for our Daddy. By chance he had picked up two long, thick pieces of wood which he thought were full of character and would look good in the garden. Plus, he knew we would use it in our games. Our Daddy showed us a side of his character which had remained hidden so far.

He shouted, *"Get off"* so loudly it made us jump. Then, he banged the wood together above Titan's head. It shocked Titan and thankfully he let go of Max. He ran back to his owner who shouted, *"There was no need for that!"* Our daddy shouted, *"Yes there was. Your dog keeps attacking other dogs. He needs sorting out!"* His face was red and he looked scary. However, we knew he was being protective like us doggies are protective of our families.

Titan's owner had made no effort to come over and drag Titan off Max. This made Max's Mummy and our Mummy and Daddy very angry. Titan's owner knew how aggressive Titan was and should have put him back on his lead when another dog was near. Titan's track record was not good. He had attacked several other dogs before.

Titan's owner did not apologise, he tried deflecting our non-doggies' outrage by saying, "*He was only playing.*"

We noticed Titan's owner was also aggressive and unfriendly. Perhaps this is why Titan is so aggressive.

We knew from Daddy's reaction what Titan had done was wrong because he had attacked and hurt Max for no reason.

Later, the penny dropped, when we remembered how Mummy and Daddy had taught us the correct way to behave. They showed us what we had done wrong, then how to correct our behaviour and then showered us with praise when we behaved well.

Perhaps Titan's owner did not do this and just allowed him to act however he wanted to. This was not good for Titan though, he had grown up into a nasty dog who thought is was acceptable to attack other dogs. He did not show any compassion for other dogs or even his owner!

That night we heard Mummy and Daddy talking. They thought we were asleep, but we knew how to pretend to be asleep. All dogs do, so we know what is going on, especially when it comes to walks and treats! They mentioned the word 'bullying'. We had not heard this word before, but when we listened to their discussion, we understood it related to Max's attack.

The next day, our Mummy and Daddy took us to see Max. They were worried about him and his Mummy because it had been a scary and horrible experience for them both. Poor old Max had some stitches in his wound and was far from his usual playful self. His poor Mummy looked very pale and tired because she had slept next to his basket to comfort him because he was so scared after the attack. She thanked our Daddy for being an Upstander.

This terrifying episode had shaken us all up. It is not right for any doggie to attack another doggie for any reason. Doggies who attack need to receive special help and attention from a professional dog counsellor.

Human Highlight

♈ *Sadly, bullying is still a problem in everyday life. It can take place anywhere; at home, at school and continue into the work place. The advent of the internet and mobile phones has introduced new methods of bullying which can sometimes be difficult to get away from. If bullying is not identified or addressed, its effects can have long-lasting consequences to health in later life.*

♈ This chapter helps children to see that bullying can be addressed when given the right support, as Apple and Maci (and their human parents) did for Max and his owner. Children can be encouraged here to talk about instances they have seen or experienced.

♈ This chapter reminds children the best thing to do is to talk about their worries with a trusted adult, friend or professional counsellor.

Sniff It Out!

🐾 How would you explain bullying?

🐾 Are there different types of bullying?

🐾 If somebody is being bullied how does their behaviour change?

🐾 What does it feel like to be bullied?

🐾 Sometimes people who are being bullied don't want to tell anyone, why do you think this is?

🐾 Are bullies bad people? Why do you think they bully others?

🐾 Apple and Maci's daddy was an Upstander, what do you think this means?

🐾 What should you do if somebody you know is being bullied?

🐾 Who does bullying happen to? Is it only to children?

Environment

Just when we thought life could not get any better, we were very pleasantly surprised. A lesson in life for us is you are never too old to enjoy new experiences.

Despite Macis' attempts to be in charge of the route, Mummy and Daddy were firm and took us on a new route to a place we had certainly not been to before. The grass was not satiny and soft, in fact, it was rough and some of the edges of the blades were sharp - we did not like it.

It looked like the soil in our garden but was a beige colour and consisted of millions of tiny grains. Our paws sunk a lot further into it than the soil in our garden - it was the same for Mummy and Daddy. The jury was out; we were not sure if we liked this place.

However, just as if this new place sensed what we were thinking, the horrible rough and sharp bladed grass disappeared and it revealed a whole new pleasure dome!

What was that noise? We had never heard anything like it before. A wall of white noise had crept up on us, then surrounded and captured us as we entered this new arena.

We stopped and listened so our ears could tune into the new channel of crashing and roaring sounds.

Shhhhh, shhhh, shhhh!

There was a pulsing element to it. We looked over to the source and were blown away by what was producing this mesmerising melody.

It looked like a sapphire jelly before it sets, still fluid and susceptible to the power of nature. The sound it made was rhythmic. It arrived smoothly, but slightly frothily, onto the beach, as if it had been poured out of a giant heavenly jug from a great height, then as if it had changed its mind, rushed back out towards the horizon.

Of course, as you might have guessed, we had another new game, which was called, *'Say hello, but don't get wet!'* Needless to say, the wet stuff won.

If Mummy and Daddy saw somebody they put us on our leads. This was so we did not jump up to say hello and make their clothes dirty with our wet and sandy paws (we did aim to greet everybody in our excitement).

They would say hello and if the person started a conversation, they would chat with them. We would always listen as we wanted to know if they were talking about us. Every one of the non-doggies looked very happy after our chats. Was this because the people had no one to talk to before meeting us?

We did have a think about this and how we would feel if we did not have each other and our doggie friends to talk to and have fun with. We loved our new special place.

There was only one thing which we did not like about our new sea and sand haven.

Litter!

It really spoilt our fun and spoilt the beauty of

this place, especially if it was plastic. We hate litter. Grrrrrr!

Our paws sometimes got caught up in it as we ran about and you could see the wet creature despised it. It would try to spit it out as it poured onto the beach.

'Where does it come from?' we wondered. We were horrified to learn some people who visit the beach and surrounding areas drop litter and are too lazy too pick it up. Then, they leave the rest of their litter behind on the beach instead of taking it home with them. There is also some rubbish from tips which gets dumped in the sea which contains plastic.

We believe plastic is the most evil litter because it survives for years and not only litters our beach but floats around in the seas and oceans and some of it you can't even see! There are even tiny balls of plastic in some toothpaste and types of creamy stuff which mummy washes her face with. These plastic balls are so tiny, sea-creatures eat them without knowing. Then we eat the sea-creatures and they end up in our tummies.

Our Mummy and Daddy have taught us what plastic looks like so we do not eat it, but our marine friends have nobody to warn them about it.

We cried with anger when our Mummy and Daddy told us thousands of our marine friends die from plastic entanglement each year and these are the ones which are found. Approximately, one million seabirds die due to plastic waste every year. A plastic bag takes a long time to biodegrade so can kill many animals over this time.

Mummy and Daddy told us all the world needs to do is to recycle their plastic rubbish and stop using plastic and synthetic products to prevent micro-plastics entering the environment and the eco-system. It's really easy - Mummy and Daddy avoid them. When there is no alternative, Mummy and Daddy recycle their plastic rubbish by simply washing it, putting it in a special plastic bag. When the bag is full, they put into their recycling bin.

Human Highlight

🚶 *Unless you have been 'off grid' for the past few years, you will be aware of the huge danger which litter, and in particular plastic, poses to our environment and ecosystem.*

🚶 *Plastic is particularly noticeable on the beach where Apple and Maci live and on beaches all around the world. The sight of golden sand, the wonderful sea and the wildlife which should give visitors a lift is marred by the rubbish which is washed up every day. The dogs think it looks like ugly, alien intruders on the beach.*

Canine Capers

✳ *This chapter provides an opportunity to discuss the environments where children live, how they differ and how they can help to improve it by simple everyday actions. Further discussions can be ventured into: about the effect we have on beaches and wildlife not just in our own environment but across the world too.*

Sniff It Out!

- *What is the seaside like?*

- *If you have been to the seaside, what did you like most about it?*

- *What did you do at the beach?*

- *How much litter did you see?*

- *What can you do to help the environment if you go to the beach?*

- *Where does plastic end up if people do not recycle it properly?*

- *What other types of pollution do you know about?*

- *How can you help the environment in your everyday life?*

Illness

Why haven't Mummy and Daddy got up yet? We don't mind, because we are perfectly comfortable in bed with them. However, it is not their usual routine and dogs always know the routine of our families!

Mind you, we did hear Mummy and Daddy coughing in the night and they were both very restless. They were hot then they were cold.

They took these tablet things because they ached all over. Also, Mummy was dressed up like a *'mummy'*, if you excuse the pun. Was it because she was cold? She usually just wears a nightdress.

We noticed other things; they did not have one of their tantalising smelling meals last night; they just threw some cereal into two bowls and added a banana for dinner. They did not sit up at the table like they usually do: but ate on the settee. Then, they both just laid there all night with blankets over them.

The fact they stayed on the settee all night did not bother us because we loved snuggling up with them. We made the most of the fact they both had blankets over them which made it even more cosy for us.

Oh, wait a minute, they are getting up, but they are not getting dressed. They are just putting on their dressing gowns. They are not even having a shower! They seem to have become weak overnight. Their steps are so slow and laboured. It is very worrying.

Obviously, we followed them, all be it more slowly than usual. Daddy went into the lounge and sat on the settee and Mummy went into the kitchen and put the kettle on. At least that was normal behaviour! We jumped up and sat with Daddy on the settee. Mummy came into the lounge with mugs of tea for them both.

We don't know why but having seen Daddy and Mummy walking so slowly and looking frail, made us want to give them even more love than normal; we decided not to pester them for our morning walk.

A clue at last; we heard Daddy on the phone. He was saying in a very hoarse voice, *"Sorry Peter, Trisha and I won't be into work today and possibly the rest of the week because we've got the 'flu."*

Then Mummy said, *"Oh Kevin, you better let Louise know we are ill, so she does not come over for dinner tomorrow night, and catch our germs."*

What is the 'flu? Why does the 'flu make Mummy and Daddy, not shower, lay on the settee and eat cereal instead of their usual yummy meals? We were all of a dither. Has our lovely routine and life to come to an end. Oh, please not!

Mummy said, *"Bless you girls, you are being very patient with us. We are so grateful to have such good girls. Mummy and Daddy are so sorry we are ill and cannot take you out for your walks, but as soon as we are better, we will take you on a lovely walk to the beach."*

Phew! This situation was only going to be temporary. What wonderful parents we have. It is frustrating to be unable to go out for walks at the moment, but it's not because they cannot be bothered; it's because Mummy said they are ill.

We put our thinking caps on as we wanted to understand what being ill was, this horrible thing had made our Mummy and Daddy so weak and frail.

Our logic told us it could be given to other people because they had cancelled their dinner with Louise. We also noticed when they coughed they put their hands over their mouths and when they blew their noses they flushed the tissue down the loo and then washed their hands.

Obviously, Mummy and Daddy wash their hands a lot, particularly after they stroke us and then prepare food. However, they seemed to be washing their hands even more often. So, we surmised: washing your hands gets rid of nasty things.

Mummy and Daddy are also sleeping a lot more than usual. Why is this? We know sleep is important, because they have told us many times we should sleep if we are tired.

Our major conundrum was with the food. Mummy and Daddy had changed their diet due to being ill. We guessed it was because they were feeling so weak, they did not have the energy to spend time in the kitchen like they usually did.

However, we had learned enough from listening to Mummy to know their cereal was healthy because it did not contain lots of sugar and they added fresh fruit, nuts and seeds to ensure they had important vitamins to help get better quicker.

Mummy and Daddy were ill for another three or four sleeps, then after having a cup of tea in bed, Daddy got up and had a shower, then Mummy got up and had a shower as well. Yippee! Mummy and Daddy are feeling better. The next step was to see if they cooked something, rather than eating cereal. They went into the kitchen and cooked boiled eggs and toast, then ate them at the table. We were so happy Mummy and Daddy were feeling better. They were not fully fit again, but definitely on the road to recovery.

Having listened to Mummy, we know health is very important. It is vital people do not go back to work before they are fully recovered. This is so their long-term health is not affected and the nasty things they get rid of when they wash their hands are not passed onto other people.

This episode in our lives of Mummy and Daddy being ill has been a revelation. We know Mummy has a different chronic illness and sometimes feels low, but there are no physical signs like coughing.

Human Highlight

♔ *We all suffer illness at some point in our lives. It is important to recognise when you (or other people) are ill and know how to look after yourself through the illness and during the recovery. This includes looking after your mental wellbeing as well as your physical health.*

♔ *This chapter provides a chance to discuss how to prevent the spread of germs which may lead to illnesses such as colds and flu; or to talk about longer term illness such as cancer or Parkinson's. It can also be a moment to consider different ways in which children can improve and boost their mental resilience.*

Sniff It Out!

🐾 *Describe a time when you were ill?*

🐾 *How did being ill make you feel?*

🐾 *What causes illnesses and how can illnesses be passed to other people?*

🐾 *How are we protected against some illnesses?*

🐾 *How does washing your hands regularly prevent the spread of illnesses?*

🐾 *Do you know any other types of illness e.g. mental illness or wellbeing related illness?*

🐾 *Do you ever have to look after a member of your family? For how long?*

🐾 *If you needed to look after someone when they were ill, what would you do?*

🐾 *How can we try to eat better when we are feeling ill and don't feel like preparing a meal?*

Domestic Violence

It was night time in our cosy nest of a home. We had assumed our usual position between Mummy and Daddy on the settee. Well, you don't expect us to sit on the floor do you?

The settee is for all of the family. If we lay between Mummy and Daddy they do not have to reach far to stroke us, which shows our level of thoughtfulness; we are all heart!

Our idyllic and blissful night was brought to an abrupt end. The doorbell rang and kept ringing. Our parents wondered who on earth it was because the noise of the doorbell was deafening.

Daddy got up to answer the door and he closed the lounge door after him to keep the heat in.

We were yanked out of our slumber because we heard Daddy saying, *"Oh my Gosh! What on earth has happened. Come on in Jill."* The lounge door reopened with Daddy walking back in with his arm around Jill. Jill's body looked weak and limp; our Daddy's arm was like a supporting and comforting brace around her.

He gently lowered her onto the settee. There was no need for Mummy and Daddy to speak because they knew something was very wrong and our instinct told us Jill was not her normal bouncy and bubbly self, so we did not demand our usual fuss and kisses from her.

Mummy eased up to her on the settee and gave her a great big hug. It was like she had thrown a protective and soft safety blanket over her. She whispered, *"What's happened Jill?"*

Jill broke down and sobbed uncontrollably. Her whole body convulsed with emotion. Mummy gently rubbed her back to try and comfort her. This went on for some time.

After what seemed ages, Jill stopped sobbing, but her poor eyes were bright red and puffy with crying, her face glistened with a deluge of tears and there was what appeared to be food smeared on her face. As if this was not bad enough, her lip looked swollen and there was blood on it.

"He hit me again," she whispered. She lifted up her top and we could see a huge bruise starting to form. You could see the horror in our Mummy's eyes. Not only had Jill's husband hit her, but it was not the first time. We knew this was not right because our Mummy and Daddy never hit us, even when we misbehave.

"Why did he hit you?" Mummy asked. Jill replied, *"He had had a bad day at work and then when I served up our dinner he said his steak was overdone. He threw his plate onto the floor, then grabbed my hair and forced me to the floor. He rubbed my face in the dinner, then lifted up my face and punched me. Then, when I fell back down to the floor, he kicked me in the stomach."*

Mummy was speechless, but Daddy looked angry. We knew Daddy would never hurt Mummy or us. He was so angry with Jill's husband, he was like a volcano full of lava and ready to erupt.

"I'll go round and sort him out!" he shouted, but then he looked at Jill and realised violence was not the answer. Jill looked exhausted; Mummy

got her a warm drink. Daddy went upstairs and got our spare room ready. Jill went to bed as soon as she had finished her drink.

Mummy and Daddy sat on the settee in silence. This was unusual for them, but we think they were feeling the shock of what had happened to poor Jill.

Mummy was the first to speak. *"What are we going to do? Should we call the Police? She can't go back home and risk being hit again."* *"I know darling."* said Daddy and took Mummy's hand. He gave it a squeeze and a kiss to show he understood how Mummy was feeling.

"I think we need to let Jill have a good night's sleep because she looks as though she has not been sleeping. Then we need to sit down with her and talk about what her plans are and how we can support her. We do not have any experience of this issue, but perhaps we can ask for advice on Jill's behalf."

"Oh darling," said Mummy to Daddy, *"I do love you. I am so relieved you are here with me so we can both support Jill."*

They then gave each other a great big hug. We just watched and glowed with admiration for our lovely parents.

Domestic Violence

Human Highlight

♟ *Domestic violence is not a new problem; but it's only since the 1960's and '70's, when women began to have more of a voice in society, that victims have felt able to speak up. This has created more support for victims and a variety of organisations are available to help. It is a difficult subject to talk about for anyone, but particularly those going through it or witnessing it.*

♟ *Apple and Maci witness the effects of domestic violence on their Mummy's friend. They learn how their Mummy and Daddy listen to her, provide support and give her a safe place to stay.*

♟ *This chapter helps to open up discussions. As children listen to the story, they can understand that talking about difficulties and abuse is the first step to receiving help. It is a good idea to let children know they don't have to talk about their worries in a big group but can have a one-to-one conversation with a trusted adult.*

Sniff It Out!

🐕 *In your own words, explain what 'upset' means?*

🐕 *What do you think makes people get upset?*

🐕 *Can you describe what people do when they are upset?*

🐕 *Have you ever seen any grown ups who are upset?*

🐕 *What would you do if you saw someone being hurt by another person?*

🐕 *What would you do if you are feeling scared or worried?*

🐕 *Who can help you if you do feel scared or worried?*

🐕 *How can you make a situation safe for yourself or others?*

🐕 *Should Apple and Maci's parents have called somebody else to help Jill?*

🐕 *What do you think 'domestic abuse' means?*

Death

What is going on? Where is Nanny and her super big chews? They are nearly as big as us! We love our Nanny. She always gives us such a warm welcome and lets us sit on her chair even though there is not really enough room for all three of us.

Nanny is just like Mummy and Daddy with us. She gives us so much love and attention. Nothing is ever too much trouble for Nanny.

She looks after us if Daddy has to go out on a job after he takes Mummy to the office. She comes out onto her verandah in her long, green dressing gown to greet us.

"Hello girls," she says and we reach up her legs and get so much lovely fuss. Grandad is usually still in bed, so we have Nanny all to ourselves. We are happy and relaxed, relishing the thought of her undivided attention for at least two hours.

We might be dogs, (although we consider ourselves to be on the same intellectual level as the non-doggies), but we know when something is wrong.

We have been over to visit Grandad several times and then have been left at Grandad's whilst Mummy and Daddy take Grandad over to the hospital to see Nanny.

We always listen to all of our family's conversations, so we know Nanny needed an operation. The word 'cancer' was mentioned. We put two and two together and realised it must be serious if Nanny needed an operation.

On this particular Saturday it was different. Mummy's sister, Auntie Tara, had arrived at Grandad's. Mummy and Daddy had taken Grandad and Tara over to see Nanny and then we all had dinner at Grandad's.

It was lovely for us to be with Mummy and

Daddy's family, even though Nanny was in hospital, but we knew everybody had visited Nanny and it must have cheered her up. We would have normally gone home, but on this night we went to bed at Grandad's.

Then, deep into the night, it happened. Daddy had just been to the bathroom and then Mummy got up, too. Whilst Mummy was in the bathroom, Auntie Tara appeared in our bedroom. We heard the words, *"The hospital has just phoned to say Mum, (our Nanny) has passed away."* We heard Daddy say, *"Oh no, I'm so sorry Tara. I'll let Trisha know."* Mummy came back from the bathroom and Daddy said, *"Trisha, I've got something to tell you,"*

We could see Mummy knew what was coming. Daddy said, *"I am so sorry, but the hospital has just phoned: your Mum has passed away."* Mummy's body went limp and Daddy held onto her. We knew their world had been shattered by this terrible news. Our wonderful Nanny, our Mummy's Mummy, had died.

Mummy and Auntie Tara went to see Grandad. He was so quiet. We do not think he believed Nanny had gone. Somehow, we all managed to get back to sleep, but then the day dawned and the horrible reality hit us like a huge punch to the stomach.

There was a sense of disbelief. Had we dreamed it? Surely Nanny had not really died?

Please tell us Nanny is still here. Sadly, as the day progressed, the very sad truth sunk in.

Why did Nanny have to die and make everybody so sad? It's not fair, she was so lovely, and we all loved her so much.

Where has she gone? Daddy told Mummy Nanny had passed away. Where has she passed to? Can't we go and get her back? It only took a split second to decide this was the worst day in our lives. We wanted to help Mummy, Daddy, Grandad and Aunty Tara, but we were not sure of the best way to do this.

After lots of thought, we remembered what Mummy had done when her friend came round and had been hurt by her husband. Mummy hugged her friend, so we worked out a rota whereby we would sit with our dear non-doggies, reach up and kiss them and snuggle up to them, which we really hoped would help them to be less sad.

Our family had no need to worry as we were here to look after them. We felt confident our love would help them. It was the least we could do after they had all given us so much love, happiness and security.

Human Highlight

✚ *Death is a difficult life event to endure. It steals your nearest and dearest from you often without warning and with no mercy. However, it is unavoidable, and everyone will experience loss at some point.*

✚ *This chapter demonstrates the tidal wave of grief which forms when a death occurs in a close-knit family like Apple and Maci's. They are themselves devastated and can see how catastrophic Nanny's death is for their family. They do not know how to help. Eventually their instincts take over and they show their family even more love and compassion than usual. They cannot talk, but their actions of love speak for themselves.*

✚ *In this chapter, the key message is: even if you don't know what to say, a hug or an act of kindness can say it all. Just being there may make it easier for the grieving person to talk about their loss if they wish. It also explores the range of feelings people have when they lose a person or pet they love.*

Sniff It Out!

🐕 *What happened to Nanny?*

🐕 *What does passed away mean?*

🐕 *Have you ever lost a pet? How did you say goodbye to them?*

🐕 *What are the reasons people die?*

🐕 *What happens when somebody dies?*

🐕 *Where do people go when they die?*

🐕 *Has somebody who you used to know died?*

🐕 *How did it make you feel?*

🐕 *How did the people around you support you?*

🐕 *What do the people left behind do to remember the person who has died?*

Epilogue

We would like to thank you for reading our story. Our aim has been to show you all whatever start you have in life, there is no reason why you should not feel happy, loved, wanted, listened to, safe and secure.

Material things and possessions are not a priority for us. It's lovely when we are given special tasty treats, new leads and even new coats in the winter, but we do not pine for these things if we do not get them.

We agree the most important areas in our life are all present and correct. Perhaps the vital elements in our lives which make us happy, are the essential features of a home.

The safety and security we feel in our home, are like the foundations in a house. If these are laid out and prepared correctly, the house will be strong and won't collapse!

In our opinion, it is how your family goes about making you feel loved and valued which is important. Good communication is vital to make all these good feelings happen. This is why we have told our story (with the help of our non-doggies). We want all families to be like ours!

We count our blessings every day. We believe it is vital everybody is grateful for what they have and do not obsess about what they do not have.

However, we understand there are some people whose life is not as happy as ours, and they may need support, so please contact the organisations in the next chapter which may help you with any concerns.

Always remember, fussing a dog can also help you feel better, (remember to ask their non-doggie if it is okay first though). It gives you an instant boost of happy hormones!

Human Highlight

♦♦♦ *Sadly, there is a lot of materialism in this world. Advertising on television, on social media and the peer-pressure to 'keep up' with other families makes it difficult to instill values such as gratitude, priviledge and kindness.*

♦♦♦ *As far as Apple and Maci are concerned, material things like new leads and coats are not important. What they want and need is unconditional love in a home where their parents talk with one another about all circumstances, including some of the challenging issues written about in this book.*

♦♦♦ *Apple and Maci would, in their very wise and down to earth way, sum it up with the two expressions, 'What the world needs now, is love, sweet love.' and 'It's good to talk.'*

Helpful Organisations

Here are a selection of organisations and charities who can help with the issues raised in this book. As a general note, if something happens and you really do not know which way to turn, then in an emergency call 'The Police' on 999. If you are not in immediate danger call 'The Samaritans' on 116 123 (they are available 365 days a year, 24/7). They will listen and then signpost you to charities who can help.

However, if the issue is important but not critically urgent, then here are some charities who may be able to help. They have been matched to the issues raised in each chapter.

Chapter 1 – Pregnancy & Birth

Best Beginnings

By providing expert support and practical help, largely through our free parenting app, *Baby Buddy*, we give parents, co-parents and caregivers the knowledge and confidence to take good care of themselves and support them to build healthy, happy lives for their children. We are here for all families, with an unwavering commitment to reducing inequalities.

www.bestbeginnings.org.uk

Phone: 020 7443 7895

New Parents Support (NCT)

Our mission is to support parents through the first 1,000 days to have the best possible experience of pregnancy, birth and early parenthood.

www.nct.org.uk

Tel: 0300 330 0700

Parents 1st

Parents 1st enables effective volunteering to help families flourish during pregnancy, birth and beyond. We want more parents and babies to benefit from peer support and the help it can provide.

www.parents1st.org.uk

Phone: 07718 494228

The Maternal Mental Health Alliance (MMHA)

A UK-wide charity and network of over 100 organisations, dedicated to ensuring women and families affected by perinatal mental problems have access to high-quality comprehensive care and support. We bring the maternal mental health community together and make change happen by combining the power of real-life experience with clinical and professional expertise.

www.maternalmentalhealthalliance.org

Email: info@maternalmentalhealthalliance

Chapter 2 and 3 – Family and Homes

Action For Children
Our parenting programmes support families and care-givers around the UK. They're designed to help parents and children bond, learn, or overcome difficulties.

www.parents.actionforchildren.org.uk

Phone: 0300 123 2112

Email: ask.us@actionforchildren.org.uk

Adoption UK
Adoption UK is the leading charity providing support, community and advocacy for all those whose lives involve adoption, including those parenting children who cannot live with their birth families, and adopted people. We connect people, provide support and training and campaign for improvements to adoption policy and practice. We provide a strong, supportive community and are the largest voice of adopters in the UK

www.adoptionuk.org

Phone: 0300 666 0006

Email: helpline@adoptionuk.org.uk

Barnardo's
Every child should grow up feeling loved and supported. Barnados provides a range of services to help and support families across the UK, working with organisations and professionals so that children get the best start in life.

www.barnardos.org.uk/adopt

Phone: 0800 008 7005

Email: supporterrelations@barnardos.org.uk

Coram

Coram has over 40 years' experience in finding permanent loving families for children needing adoption. We support families through the adoption process and beyond, and we are highly experienced in helping new adoptive families adjust.

www.coramadoption.org.uk

Phone: 020 7520 0383

Email: adoption@coram.org.uk

Family Action

Family Action works to tackle some of the most complex and difficult issues facing families today – including financial hardship, mental health problems, social isolation, learning disabilities, domestic abuse, substance misuse and alcohol problems.

www.family-action.org.uk

Phone: 0808 802 6666

Text: 07537 404 282

Email: familyline@family-action.org.uk

Families Need Fathers

FNF is the leading UK charity supporting dads, mums and grandparents to have personal contact and meaningful relationships with their children following parental separation.

www.fnf.org.uk

Phone: 0300 0300 363

Forum: www.fnf.org.uk/forum/

Gingerbread

We are the leading national charity working with single parent families. Since 1918, we have been at the forefront of shaping policy and services that support single parents. Today, there are two million single parent families in the country. We champion their voices and keep their needs at the heart of everything we do.

www.gingerbread.org.uk

Phone: 0808 802 0925

Email: peersupport@gingerbread.org.uk

Home-Start

Home-Start works with families in communities right across the UK. Starting in the home, our approach is as individual as the people we're helping. No judgement, it is just compassionate, confidential help and expert support.

www.home-start.org.uk

Phone: 0116 464 5490

Email: info@home-start.org.uk

Relate

We're the UK's largest provider of relationship support, and last year we helped over two million people of all ages, backgrounds, sexual orientations and gender identities to strengthen their relationships. Find out more about what we do and how we can help you on our website.

www.relate.org.uk

Contact: See the website for your local Relate centre or the Live Help Virtual Assistant.

TACT Fostering

Our core remit is to provide high-quality, child-centred fostering services. However, we also campaign on behalf of children in care, carers and families.

www.tactcare.org.uk

Phone: Tel: 0330 123 2250

The Centre for Separated Families

Practical information for parents who are sharing care, those who are caring for their children alone and those who are not able to spend time with their children. Parents, carers, grandparents or anyone else with concerns about family separation are welcome.

www.separatedfamilies.info

Voices in The Middle

Voices in the Middle is a collaboration between young people, the family law & mediation sector and The Family Initiative charity to provide a dedicated place for young people to find help and support when in the middle of divorce and separation.

www.voicesinthemiddle.com

Contact: Online only – Hit the *Find Help* Button

Chapter 4 – Walking and Keeping Active

Living Streets

Living Streets is the UK charity for everyday walking. We want a nation where walking is the natural choice for everyday local journeys. Our mission is to achieve a better walking environment and inspire people to walk more.

www.livingstreets.org.uk

Phone: 020 7377 4900

Email: info@livingstreets.org.uk

Sport In Mind

We are the UK's leading mental health sports charity and deliver physical activity (sport, walking, dance and movement, gardening and exercise sessions) projects in partnership with the amazing NHS in order to aid recovery, promote mental wellbeing, improve physical health, combat social isolation and empower people to move their lives forward in a positive direction.

www.sportinmind.org

Phone: 0118 947 9762

Email: info@sportinmind.org

UK Active

Our long-standing and uncompromising vision is to get more people, more active, more often. We are committed to improving the health of the nation through promoting active lifestyles.

www.ukactive.com

Phone: 020 8158 9700

Email: info@ukactive.org.uk

Chapter 5 - Food

Beat

We are the UK's eating disorder charity. Founded in 1989 as the Eating Disorders Association, our mission is to end the pain and suffering caused by eating disorders.

www.beateatingdisorders.org.uk

Phone: 0808 801 0677

Email: help@beateatingdisorders.org.uk

British Nutrition Foundation

Connecting people, food and science, for better nutrition and healthier lives. We work with experts across the nutrition and food community to provide impartial, evidence-based information, education and expertise, motivating people to adopt healthy, sustainable diets – for life.

www.nutrition.org.uk

Phone: 020 7557 7930

Eating Disorder Hope™

Eating Disorder Hope™ is an online community that offers resources, education, support, and inspiration to those struggling with anorexia nervosa, bulimia nervosa, binge eating disorder, body image issues, and a myriad of other disordered eating behaviors and their families.

www.eatingdisorderhope.com

Contact: for online help, please visit the website

Food Foundation
Our mission is changing food policy and business practice to ensure everyone, across our nation, can afford and access a healthy diet.

www.foodfoundation.org.uk

Phone: 020 3086 9953

Email: office@foodfoundation.org.uk

Chapter 6 – Bullying

Act Against Bullying

Act Against Bullying was formed in 2000, due to concerns about the escalation of bullying in the UK. Our mission is to be able to provide under 18's with practical advice if they are being bullied.

www.actagainstbullying.org

Contact: Use the online form for help and advice.

Anti-Bullying Alliance

We are a unique coalition of organisations and individuals, working together to achieve our vision to: stop bullying and create safer environments in which children and young people can live, grow, play and learn.

www.anti-bullyingalliance.org.uk

Email: aba@ncb.org.uk

Help With Bullying

Our vision is for all children to grow up in supportive communities safe from bullying and harm. Our mission is to provide practical support, training and advice to challenge bullying and protect young lives.

www.kidscape.org.uk

Email: info@kidscape.org.uk

National Bullying Helpline

The UK's only charitable organisation addressing Adult Bullying and Child Bullying. Our Mission is to continue to work towards eradicating anti-social behaviour in all corners or our society and occasionally that involves campaigning, speaking out and raising awareness.

www.nationalbullyinghelpline.co.uk

Phone: 0300 323 0169

Email: help@nationalbullyinghelpline.co.uk

StandUp Foundation

The StandUp Foundation, founded by Ben Cohen, is the world's first foundation dedicated to raising awareness of the long-term, damaging effects of bullying by connecting communities and raising funds to support those doing real-world work to eradicate bullying.

www.standupfoundation-uk.org

Email: info@bcsuf.co.uk

Young Minds

We're the UK's leading charity fighting for children and young people's mental health. We want to see a world where no young person feels alone with their mental health issues, and all young people get the mental health support they need, when they need it, no matter what.

www.youngminds.org.uk

Phone: 0202 7089 5050

Chapter 7 - Pollution

CleanUpUK

CleanupUK is a charity that unites volunteers to bring about cleaner, connected and safer urban and rural communities by tackling the litter problems where they live. Cleaning up and litter-picking are activities which bring people closer together, enable neighbours to meet one another other and help create a greater sense of pride and community in local areas.

www.cleanupuk.org.uk

Email: info@cleanupuk.org.uk

Keep Britain Tidy

Keep Britain Tidy is an independent charity with three goals – to eliminate litter, end waste and improve places. This means more to us than just picking up litter. It means creating clean beaches, parks and streets. It means creating sustainable practices and eliminating unnecessary waste.

www.keepbritaintidy.org

Email: enquiries@keepbritaintidy.org

Marine Conservation Society

We are the Marine Conservation Society, a UK charity fighting for a cleaner, better-protected, healthier ocean: one we can all enjoy.

www.mcsuk.org/about-us

Phone: 01989 566017

Email: info@mcsuk.org

Sea Shepherd UK

Sea Shepherd UK is a registered marine conservation charity. Its primary mission is to end the destruction of habitats and illegal killing of wildlife around the UK's coastline and across the world's oceans in order to conserve and protect marine ecosystems and species.

www.seashepherd.org.uk

Phone: 0300 111 0501

Email: volunteer@seashepherduk.org

Chapter 8 – Illness

Carnegie UK

At Carnegie UK we're all about wellbeing. We have been ever since we were set up over 100 years ago. Wellbeing has meant different things to different generations. Right now, the world around us is changing in ways that mean it is time to rethink how we help people to live well together.

www.carnegieuktrust.org.uk

Phone: 01383 721445

Email: info@carnegieuk.org

Honeypot

We are the national young carers' charity. Our countryside respite breaks and range of support services give young carers, with responsibilities beyond their years, the chance to be a child again. Because you only get one chance of a happy, fulfilling childhood.

www.honeypot.org.uk

Phone: 020 7602 2631

Email: info@honeypot.org.uk

Kaleidoscope+ Group

At The Kaleidoscope Plus Group, our goal is to champion mental health and wellbeing, driving real change and providing crucial mental health support services to the community, wherever they are needed.

www.kaleidoscopeplus.org.uk

Phone: 0121 565 5605

Mental Health UK

Mental Health UK brings together the heritage and experience of four charities from across the country who've been supporting people with their mental health for nearly 50 years.

www.mentalhealth-uk.org

Phone: 0121 522 7007

Email: info@rethink.org

Mind

We provide advice and support to empower anyone experiencing a mental health problem. We campaign to improve services, raise awareness and promote understanding. We have a new campaign: The Mind Walk – a 10km walk through Central London – to raise funds for our cause.

www.mind.org.uk

Phone: 0300 123 3393

Email: info@mind.org.uk

The Children's Society

Young carers are children who look after a friend or family member. Their extra responsibilities often mean they miss out on school and hanging out with friends. It can sideline their whole childhood. We help them find balance, give them space to enjoy being young and support them into adulthood so they can pursue their dreams outside of caring.

www.childrenssociety.org.uk

Phone: 0300 303 7000

Email: supportercare@childrenssociety.org.uk

Chapter 9 - Domestic Abuse

Police

If you have, or are experiencing domestic violence then getting help is perhaps the most important thing you can do. In an emergency, call 999. If it is not an emergency, you could contact your local police station and discuss your situation with them.

www.police.uk

Phone: 999 (Emergencies only)

IDAS

IDAS is the largest specialist charity in Yorkshire supporting anyone experiencing or affected by domestic abuse or sexual violence.

Our services include refuge accommodation, community based support, peer mentoring, group work and access to a free, confidential out of hours' helpline.

www.idas.org.uk

Phone: 03000 110 110 / 0808 808 2241

Email: info@idas.org.uk

National Centre for Domestic Violence

Our mission is to help people identify the early signs of domestic abuse, make decisions for a better life and to make domestic abuse socially unacceptable.

www.ncdv.org.uk

Phone: 0800 970 2070

Text: NCDV to 60777

Email: office@ncdv.org.uk

Refuge

At Refuge, we believe that no-one should have to live in fear of violence and abuse. On any given day Refuge supports more than 6,000 clients, helping them rebuild their lives and overcome many different forms of violence and abuse; for example domestic violence, sexual violence, controlling and coercive behaviour, human trafficking and modern slavery, and female genital mutilation. Refuge has links to The National Domestic Abuse Helpline which has a 24 hour free phone helpline providing advice and support to women and can refer them to emergency accommodation.

www.refuge.org.uk

Phone: 0800 2000 247

The Dash Charity

We provide specialist support to adults and children experiencing mental health issues, modern slavery, immigration, trafficking, homelessness and complex needs associated with Domestic Abuse, empowering them to live a life beyond crisis and ensuring their voices are heard.

www.thedashcharity.org.uk

Phone: 01753 549865

Solace Women's Aid

A world where everyone is able to live safe and independent lives which are free from gender-based violence, abuse and exploitation. Solace exists to end the harm done through gender-based violence. Our aim is to work to prevent violence and abuse as well as providing services to meet the individual needs of survivors particularly women and children. Our work is holistic and empowering, working alongside survivors to achieve independent lives free from abuse.

www.solacewomensaid.org

Phone: 0808 802 5565

Email: advice@solacewomensaid.org

Helpful Organisations

Women's Aid

Women's Aid is a grassroots federation working together to provide life-saving services and build a future where domestic violence is not tolerated.

www.womensaid.org.uk

Email: helpline@womensaid.org.uk

Chapter 10 - Bereavement

Children's Bereavement Centre

The Children's Bereavement Centre is run by a committed team of friendly, supportive and professional people who are passionate about helping children and young people to cope with the grieving process brought on by the death or terminal illness diagnosis that has a prognosis of a year or less for survival of someone close.

www.childrensbereavementcentre.co.uk

Phone: 01636 551 739

Email: info@childrensbereavementcentre.co.uk

Childhood Bereavement Network

The Childhood Bereavement Network (CBN) is a specialist membership organisation, working together to support bereaved children and young people.

www.childhoodbereavementnetwork.org.uk

Phone: 0800 0288840

CRUSE

They offer support through their website, national helpline, live chat, group, zoom, telephone or one-to-one in person support. They want to make sure everyone grieving gets the help they need in a way that works for them.

www.cruse.org.uk

Phone: 0800 808 1677

Grief Encounter

One child in every UK classroom will experience the death of someone close by the time they reach 16 years old. Grief Encounter is here to help with the confusion, fear, loneliness and pain, providing a lifeline to children and young people to cope with free, immediate, one-to-one support.

www.griefencounter.org.uk

Phone: 0808 802 0111

Email: grieftalk@griefencounter.org.uk

Sands

Sands is a UK charity that works across the country to support anyone affected by the death of a baby; improve the care bereaved parents receive from health care and other professionals; and reduce the number of babies who do die by funding research and working closely with other organisations to create a world where fewer babies die.

www.sands.org.uk

Phone: 0808 164 3332

Email: helpline@sands.org.uk

Winston's Wish

Winston's Wish is a national charity that provides bereavement support, guidance and information to children and young people and their families after the death of someone close to them. We offer a range of practical support via a Freephone Helpline, online resources, individual and group support, publications, and training for professionals.

www.winstonswish.org

Phone: 0808 8020 021

Email: ask@winstonswish.org

Other Useful Charities

Little Lives UK

Little Lives UK's primary focus is to help children who are disabled or disadvantaged. We provide support and opportunities to children who are facing many challenges in their young lives and are in need of support.

www.littlelives.org.uk

Phone: 020 8248 5590

Citizens Advice

We can all face problems that seem complicated or intimidating. At Citizens Advice we believe no one should have to face these problems without good quality, independent advice. We give people the knowledge and the confidence they need to find their way forward – whoever they are, and whatever their problem.

www.citizensadvice.org.uk

Phone: 0800 1448848

Animal Charities

Dogs Trust

Our mission is to bring about the day when all dogs can enjoy a happy life, free from the threat of unnecessary distress and suffering.

www.dogstrust.org.uk

Phone: 020 7837 0006

Email: info@dogstrust.org.uk

Jack Russell Terrier Rescue UK

Our mission is to save Jack Russell Terrier's from pounds, abandonment, mistreatment. We also rescue and rehome unwanted Jack Russells throughout the UK. Although we are dedicated to Jack Russell Terriers, we do help unwanted, homeless and abused dogs of all breeds.

www.jackrussellterrierrescueuk.org

Phone: 07453 261416

Email: enquiries@jackrussellterrierrescue.org

PDSA

PDSA is a charity. We want a lifetime of wellbeing for every pet. Every day, vets in our 48 Pet Hospitals care for sick and injured pets – saving lives and keeping pets happy and healthy.

www.pdsa.org.uk

Phone: 0800 917 2509

RSPCA

The Royal Society for the Prevention of Cruelty to Animals (RSPCA) and we've been here for animals since 1824. We're the world's oldest and largest animal welfare charity, with the primary focus of rescuing, rehabilitating and rehoming or releasing animals across England and Wales.

www.rspca.org.uk

Phone: 0300 1234 999

Helpful Organisations

If you speak to anyone who really helps you from any of these charities – use this space to note down their name and direct line number (if they have one).

This way you may cut down waiting time should you need to call again. They may also refer you to other people who could help.

_____

_____

_____

_____

_____

_____

_____

_____

_____

_____

_____

_____

_____

_____

_____

_____

_____

About the Author

Sally Hurst is a fantastic, free spirited individual who has a passion for wildlife and the environment. She lives in Lincolnshire, by the coast and enjoys long walks with her husband, Phil, and their two Jack Russells, Apple and Maci.

She has enjoyed writing her first book and is keen for teachers and parents around the world to get talking to their children about the difficult topics in life.

Writing Canine Capers has been a colourful contrast to her work life roles of helping businesses with their utilities and green energy solutions as 'Energy Matters' and forming two networking groups.

Both networking groups help businesses in Lincolnshire. 'Embracing Skegness' is the networking arm of the Skegness Area Business Chamber and 'Catena Lincs', is her countywide networking group.

All of her work and her writing have one thing in common; their aim of helping people.

After 35 years of working '9-5' in offices where her free spirit was reigned in, it is now free to soar to new heights for the good of her community and her local businesses.

Sally is very grateful for her new happy life with her eclectic mix of businesses and creativity and would like to thank her husband, her sister and her two Jack Russells for their love and support.

If you would like to know more about Energy Matters or the Catena Network please visit her sites at the following web addresses:-

www.energy-matters.me.uk

www.catena-business-network.com/home

Jack Russell Traits and Behaviour

Being the proud Mum of two Jack Russells transports the true meaning of 'The power of love' into reality. There is no energy more pure than unconditional love.

Perhaps it is the warmth produced by the force of true love between a dog and its owner which radiates out and melts down barriers when meeting and communicating with people.

Unconditional love must be respected and reciprocated. If you are considering getting any breed of dog it is essential you are aware of their inherent traits and ensure they are suited to your family and lifestyle. With that in mind here are some words of advice from a Jack Russell owner to anyone considering getting a 'Jack'.

General

They are lively and bouncy dogs who can make great family pets, but they will need plenty of training, guidance and attention from their owners along the way. They are affectionate, loyal, curious, intelligent, sensitive and have endless energy. They are classified as a small dog, so are perfect for small homes.

Exercise

One hour per day exercise is recommended to keep them healthy so that they live to their 12+ years expected life span. This can be divided into shorter walks over the day.

Jack Russells love to chase! They are quick and agile so you might find your Jack Russell will chase anything they see that looks like a bit of fun. It's important to ensure your garden is secure, as they can squeeze through the smallest of gaps.

Barking

Jack Russells are known for being very vocal. They tend to bark when they are excited (which is most of the time). It's important to train them early to reduce excessive barking and ensure your dog is getting enough exercise to calm them down. If you're having a problem with excessive barking it is recommended to seek the advice of a professional trainer.

Training

Jack Russells are clever dogs who respond well to encouragement for good behaviour from a young age. They pick up on new commands easily and training is a really great way to keep their busy minds active. Be consistent with training and make sure the whole household follows the same rules.

It's important to socialise your Jack Russell with lots of different people, dogs and experiences at a young age. They can be confident little dogs and this will help them to grow into a happy adult dog.

As Jack Russells are people orientated, they can suffer with separation anxiety if left alone for long periods. You'll need to train your dog to be alone, but it's recommended not to leave them alone for more than four hours.

So, households where owners work away from home and children are at school all day are not ideal.

Grooming

Jack Russell Terriers come in smooth-coated and wire-haired varieties. Both varieties moult all year round, so if you do not like dog hairs on your clothes, upholstery and carpets, they are not for you.

Brushing will help, but longer haired terriers may need to have their coats professionally groomed in the summer to keep them cool, neat and tidy.

Jack Russell Terriers and Children

Jack Russells can make good family pets if they have been trained and socialised properly from a young age. They can be less tolerant with younger or boisterous children and have been known to show their frustration by nipping. They're better suited to families with slightly older children who understand how to behave around dogs. As they are excitable, they can get more wound up if an equally excitable child is around. Remember to make sure you can recognise your dog's body language so you can put a stop to any potentially stressful situations before they escalate. Always supervise your dog with children and vulnerable adults.

A final note from me: 'WATCH OUT! Once you get a Jack, you never go back'.

In Memoriam

This book is dedicated to my Mum, Sheila, who was the most selfless person I have ever known.

The entry music at her funeral was '*Wind Beneath My Wings*' sung by *Daniel O'Donnell*, because she was always there for us as a family and always put us before herself.

She was born just three days after World War II began and her upbringing was much like other children brought up in the 1940's.

My Mum and her siblings never went hungry, were always dressed smartly and outwardly looked well cared for. They even went up to Scotland on the famous steam train, '*The Flying Scotsman*' to visit their mum's family during Summer holidays.

However, as the war inflicted rationing of vital commodities, she was starved of affection and conversation by her parents, especially as her mother suffered from severe depression.

This sad state of affairs continued until she left home to live with other family members who had ostracised her mum due to the ignorance about mental health at the time. Thankfully, she met my Father soon after and they fell in love. Then, my sister and I came along.

My sister and I were blessed with a great childhood in a happy home, but due to our mum's early years, her ability to express affection and to talk about things never blossomed.

She learned how to express her affection in other ways, but sadly for us, found it hard to give us a hug, express her feelings or talk about her worries for herself or us.

Despite having a happy family life, she would bottle up her emotions which meant in her later life, she would compensate with alcohol to numb the pain.

I NEVER want anybody else to go through the experience my Mum did, this is why I have written this book.

Dogs not only show the kind of unconditional love to their owners, like my Mum did to my sister and I, they are ice breakers who can encourage people to talk to each other.

It has been a great honour for me to write this book for my Mum, who is hopefully looking fondly down on us as I write, so for her sake, please take time to read this with your family and just take time to talk to each other.

Endorsements

"In today's busy and stressful world it can be difficult to find time to sit down and talk about day to day events. It's even harder to find the right time, place and opening gambits to have life's more difficult conversations. This book provides a great starting point, especially for parents and guardians to discuss the more tricky, emotional issues that don't come with set answers. Use this book by finding the relevant chapter that tackles an issue that has occurred for friends or family or work through each chapter so that you have discussed a whole range of potential issues in preparations for life's dilemmas. Let's start talking about life and all its highs and lows."

Clare Wildman,
Mindvalley Certified Life Coach by Evercoach

"What an ingenious vehicle for observing and interpreting healthy and unhealthy adult behaviors. It will undoubtedly engage and influence children in a really positive way. Well done Sally, Apple and Maci."

Julian Hall,
Founder of Calm People

"This book is an essential resource for teachers and pastoral teams in schools to help broach difficult topics with children known to have difficult home situations and for those who have a healthy home life"

Abbirose Adey,
Primary School Teacher

Your Thoughts

As you read the chapters, you may feel the desire to jot down any thoughts or feelings you have about each topic. If you find it difficult to talk about challenging or painful subjects, the act of writing them down may provide you comfort or help you to process your emotions.

You may even wish to show your nearest and dearest your thoughts in writing as the first step of asking for help.

Apple, Maci and I wish you a long and happy life.

_____

_____

_____

_____

_____

_____

_____

Canine Capers

_____

_____

_____

_____

_____

_____

_____

_____

_____

_____

_____

_____

_____

_____

_____

_____

_____

_____

_____

_____

Your Thoughts

_____

_____

_____

_____

_____

_____

_____

_____

_____

_____

_____

_____

_____

_____

_____

_____

_____

_____

_____

_____

_____
_____
_____
_____
_____
_____
_____
_____
_____
_____
_____
_____
_____
_____
_____
_____
_____
_____
_____
_____
_____

Your Thoughts

Printed in Great Britain
by Amazon